Pirates

Pirate Patch

and the

Gallant Rescue

In which the brave
Pirate Patch mounts
a gallant rescue to
save the kidnapped
Granny Peg

For Joshua
R.I.

For Eirrin
N.R.

Reading Consultant: Prue Goodwin, Lecturer in Literacy and
Children's Books at the University of Reading

ORCHARD BOOKS
338 Euston Road, London NW1 3BH
Orchard Books Australia
Hachette Children's Books
Level 17/207 Kent Street, Sydney NSW 2000

First published by Orchard Books in 2008
First paperback publication 2009

Text © Rose Impey 2008
Illustrations © Nathan Reed 2008

A CIP catalogue record for this book is available from the British Library

ISBN 978 1 84362 975 7 (hardback)
ISBN 978 1 84362 983 2 (paperback)

1 3 5 7 9 10 8 6 4 2
Printed in China

Orchard Books is a division of Hachette Children's Books,
an Hachette Livre UK company.
www.hachettelivre.co.uk

Pirate Patch

and the

Gallant Rescue

ROSE IMPEY • NATHAN REED

ORCHARD BOOKS

Patch was in a bad mood.
He couldn't wait until he was
a *proper* pirate.

"Pirates shouldn't have to go to school," he grumbled. But suddenly Patch stopped grumbling – something was wrong.

Pierre *wasn't* on his perch. Portside *wasn't* waiting at the gate. And Granny Peg *wasn't* digging holes in the garden as usual.

On the table was a ransom note.

Bring us the
Treasure Map...
or your GRANNY is FISH FOOD!

Signed: Your sworn enemies

"It's from Bones and Jones,"
Patch growled.
"That *scurvy* pair!"

Patch untied his crew and
picked up the treasure map.
Then he and his crew set sail
in *The Little Pearl* to
rescue Granny Peg.

In a few flaps of Pierre's wings,
they found Peg, tied up on
a sandbank.

They were only just in time.
The tide was creeping closer
by the minute.

Patch was a brave little pirate. He didn't stop for a minute before mounting a *Gallant Rescue*.

It was a pity Patch didn't stop, because the minute he left his ship . . .

. . . the *villainous* Bones and Jones crept aboard.

The cunning pair quickly sailed
away in Patch's ship, taking Peg's
map with them. They left Patch
and Peg stranded.

As *The Little Pearl* disappeared,
Patch shouted all the things he
would do when he caught up
with those pesky pirates.

Back on board *The Little Pearl*,
Bones and Jones were already
fighting about who should have
the map.

While, below deck, Portside,
the cleverest sea dog ever to sail
the seven seas, was hiding.

He was busy making a clever plan.

Suddenly Bones and Jones heard *strange* noises coming from below: "Whooo! Whooo!"

They stopped fighting over the
map. They started fighting
instead over who should go
below to investigate.

In the end, the scurvy pair went together. They opened the cabin door and peered nervously inside. But it was too dark to *see* anything.

Wh°o°o°o°o°o°o°!

G-g-great gannets!

22

The noises were getting louder.
"This ship's h-h-haunted!" they
both h-h-howled.

The next moment a ghostly white shape shot between the pirates' legs. It was wailing and whining.

Bones and Jones were so scared
they jumped overboard. They
swam for the shore – followed
by a shoal of sharks.

Then Portside, that clever sea dog,
sailed back to the sandbank.
He was just in time to rescue
Patch and Granny Peg!

"Wait till I get hold of those cheating good-for-nothings!" yelled Patch.

But that adventure would have
to wait for another day. Mum
and Dad's ship was just coming
round the headland.

Patch had to get home before they knew he'd been gone.

"How was school?" asked Dad.
"I hope you've been good,"
said Mum.

Patch smiled and nodded and looked more like a little angel than a little pirate.
If Mum and Dad only knew . . .

Pirate Patch

ROSE IMPEY NATHAN REED

All priced at £8.99

Orchard Colour Crunchies are available from all good bookshops,
or can be ordered direct from the publisher:
Orchard Books, PO BOX 29, Douglas IM99 1BQ
Credit card orders please telephone 01624 836000
or fax 01624 837033 or visit our internet site: www.orchardbooks.co.uk
or e-mail: bookshop@enterprise.net for details.

To order please quote title, author and ISBN
and your full name and address.
Cheques and postal orders should be made payable to 'Bookpost plc.'
Postage and packing is FREE within the UK
(overseas customers should add £2.00 per book).

Prices and availability are subject to change.

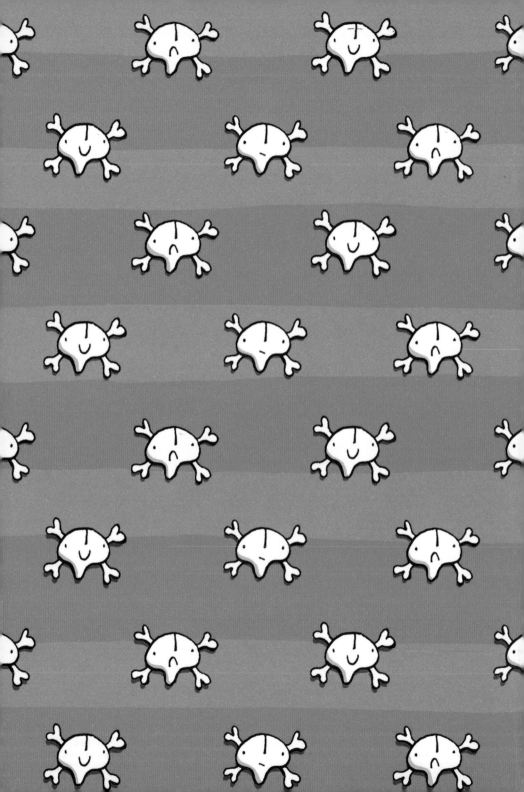